WOLVES
FOR KIDS

AMAZING FACTS AND TRUE
STORIES ABOUT THE
GRAY WOLF AND ARCTIC WOLF

Table of Contents

INTRODUCTION

Wolves for Kids is a book jam-packed with fun facts about wolves, including information on what they eat, how they live in family packs, what they look like, and where they live! This book also discusses many other things about wild animals that kids will love to learn about.

Children will learn all of the basics they need to know about wolves. They will learn about their body parts, how many exist in different habitats worldwide, and more! Kids will also explore all kinds of information on the history of wolves and where they live today.

The first chapter of this book discusses the classification of wolves, mentioning their order, family, genus, and the three main species. The chapter focuses on Canis lupus, the gray wolf, and talks about the differences and characteristics of each wolf species. The second chapter is all about the Arctic wolf, which is smaller than other wolves and has adapted to living in colder climates. The next chapter covers the wide variety of habitats for wolves to live and thrive. The last few chapters focus on how wolves are depicted in myths and legends.

Children love animals – and love learning about them. Wolves, as a species, can be incredibly fun to learn about and enjoy. They are an important part of the animal kingdom, and their numbers have been declining over time. This book is an excellent choice for young readers who want to learn about the exciting world of wolves, packed with amazing facts, beautiful images, and a wealth of knowledge.

Chapter 1: The Gray Wolf

The wolf is part of the *Canidae family*, which are *predatory dogs*. They're in the order Carnivora, which means they're meat-eating mammals. Wolves are carnivores whose diet consists of elk, moose, bison, deer, and even beavers – and are distinguished by their thick necks and narrow muzzles. This chapter will tell you all about this species' classification, description, size, population, and conservation status.

Classification of Wolves

There are three main species of wolves.

The gray wolf, known for its gray coat with a white underside, is found in Europe and most of North America.

The red wolf's coat is brownish-gray with reddish legs and sides. They live in the southeastern United States, where they're considered endangered.

The third species is the Arctic wolf, found in northern Canada and Alaska. The Arctic wolf has thick fur that helps it handle the cold weather better.

The Gray Wolf

The gray wolf, the most common wolf, lives in nearly every part of North America. They are considered a risk to livestock (chicken and sheep, for example) and are often hunted when they pose a threat to humans. They are also often hunted because they prey on moose, deer, and elk that hunters want to catch. Because of this and other factors, the gray wolf is considered an endangered species.

The Appearance of a Gray Wolf

The gray wolf's pelt is a mix of dark and light fur, which creates a gray look. The throat and belly are white, while the fur on the back is dark brown or black. The wolf has a bushy tail and large paws with strong claws. The average gray wolf stands three feet tall and weighs between 55 and 110 pounds. They have shorter fur in summer and thicker coat in winter to handle the cold. Researchers have found that a wolf's teeth and jaws are strong enough to crush bone. The canine teeth can be up to 2.5 inches long!

The gray wolf's body knows how to adapt to severe freezing conditions.

The Gray Wolf

Subspecies of the Gray Wolf

The gray wolf is part of the *Canis lupus* species, and there are over 41 different subspecies. You can tell the different subspecies apart by physical characteristics, behavior, location, and other factors. Some subspecies of the gray wolf are found in the Alps, Spain, Vietnam, and North America. The size of a wolf can change depending on where it lives. The Mexican and North American gray wolves were hunted almost to extinction and ranged from the Arctic Circle south into Mexico. The Eastern wolf has a larger body and is found in Canada and the Northern United States. The gray wolf is also found in parts of Asia, Europe, and North Africa.

The Lifespan of the Gray Wolf

Gray wolves usually live between seven and ten years in the wild but can live up to fifteen years in captivity. There are many dangers to wolves, including hunting by humans. In the wild, only a third of wolf pups survive their first year because they are prey for animals like cougars, grizzly bears, coyotes, and bobcats. They are also prey for hunters who shoot wolves when they start to attack domesticated animals.

Gray Wolf Population and Conservation Status

In 2021, according to the North American-based National Wildlife Federation, there could be as many as 40,000 gray wolves living in the United States alone. In Canada, the gray wolf population has increased to about 10,000. Unfortunately, the gray wolf is still considered an endangered species and does not have enough protection from the government. The gray wolf is very important to the ecosystem because they keep the population of deer, elk, and moose balanced. This prevents overpopulation which could lead to overgrazing and overeating of important food sources.

Yellowstone Park is actually home to a beautiful pack of Gray wolves, also known as the Gibbon wolf pack.

Wolf Pack

Fun Facts about Gray Wolves

The wolves live in packs, with alpha males and females, along with their pups. The rest of the pack is made up of beta wolves. Each wolf pack has a territory that they claim as their home. To communicate with each other, the wolves howl. They are also one of the few species that work together to take down large prey. Here are some fun facts about gray wolves:

1. A wolf can jump as high as 30 inches in the air, which is higher than some basketball players can jump!

2. A wolf can run as fast as 40 miles per hour, making them the fastest land mammal in North America.

3. Gray wolves can eat 30 pounds of meat in one meal.

4. Gray wolves howl to communicate with each other, especially during the mating season.

5. When a male and female mate, they remain together for life.

6. Gray wolves have a complicated language of fifteen different sounds.

7. When a gray wolf is howling, it can be heard from over six miles away!

8. A pack of gray wolves usually has between six and ten members but can be as large as 20.

9. When gray wolves make a kill, they will eat as much as possible – and then bury the leftovers.

10. A gray wolf's howl has been described as sounding like the wind or a person crying.

Wolf Howling

What Did We Learn?

! Wolves are one of the most unique and interesting animals in the world because they are intelligent, social creatures.

! The size of a wolf can change depending on where it lives.

! The North American gray wolf has about 40,000 wolves living in the United States alone, but they are still considered endangered.

! Gray wolves communicate with each other through howls.

! They live and hunt in packs.

! They live for 7 to 10 years in the wild!

The Arctic wolf is a subspecies of the Graywolf. It is commonly referred to as an ice or snow wolf and lives in the Arctic regions, such as Canada and Alaska. It is smaller than other gray wolves and has many adaptations that allow it to thrive in the cold. This includes a dense and water-resistant coat, small ears and tail, large paws for extra insulation, and fur between the toes to reduce slipping on snow and ice.

The Appearance of the Arctic Wolf

The Arctic wolf is much smaller than other Gray wolves, and it measures around 28-38 inches in length and weighs between 60 and 175 pounds. A male Arctic wolf can weigh 100-170 pounds, while a female weighs 60-100 pounds. Their height is around 28 inches, while they are about 38 inches long.

Many of the majestic Arctic wolves have a beautiful coat of white fur.

Arctic Wolf

Their fur has a gray or brown coat that darkens as winter approaches. A white patch of fur on each cheek and a thick white ruff at their neck help them to further camouflage in the snow. Their coat is thicker in the winter months for added warmth.

It has a thick fur coat in shades of white or cream with black markings on its face, legs, and tail tip. The fur on the bottom side of their paws is light-colored, and it keeps them warm when they walk through snow and ice. Their ears are also small compared to other subspecies of the gray wolf. They are also shorter and rounded at the tips, helping them stay warm in their cold environment. Their tails are short and bushy with a black tip.

The Lifestyle of the Arctic Wolf

Arctic wolves are social animals that live in packs of 3-11. They live in a territory ranging from 50 to 1,000 square miles and will defend their territory against intruders. They are mainly nocturnal (hunt at night) but will hunt during the day in the summer months.

Howling Arctic Wolf

9

acks consist of dominant (the big boss) and submissive (the followers) members. The alpha male and female are the dominant animals in the pack, while the omega wolf is the lowest ranking member. They communicate using both visual and vocal signals. They use their tail, body, head movements, and howling to communicate and stay in touch with other packs over great distances.

Like the Gray wolf, the Arctic wolf is a carnivore. They mainly hunt animals like rabbits and mice and eat grasses and berries in the summer months. They hunt alone by stalking their prey and using the white camouflage in their coat to sneak up on them. The Arctic wolf will eat its prey immediately or store it under the snow for later.

Arctic Wolf Pack

The Lifespan of the Arctic Wolf

Arctic wolves live about five years in the wild and up to 13 years i
captivity. They mature around two years old and will mate once
year. They give birth during March and April, with an average of :
to 10 pups in a litter. Pups are born blind and deaf with short brow
fur. They will stay with their mothers until they reach youn
adulthood (around two years old). The pack helps raise the pup
and keep them warm with the help of their dens.

Fun Facts about the Arctic Wolf

Arctic wolves are mostly nocturnal and hunt by stalking their prey
Many people believe they may have been the inspiration for storie
about werewolves. They also have some super abilities not found i
other wolves! Here are some interesting facts about Arcti
wolves:

!   Their claws can measure up to an inch long and help them ru
     over snow and ice.

!   They can run as fast as 31 miles per hour and swim for up t
     60 miles.

!   It takes about 15 minutes for an Arctic wolf to eat its pre
     after being caught.

!   The Arctic wolf is also known as the *white wolf* or *polar wolf*

!   The Arctic wolf is one of the few animals that can se
     ultraviolet light.

!   The Arctic wolf is known as a "Super Wolf" because of it
     strength and endurance.

!   In Inuit tradition, the Arctic wolf is a symbol of self
     knowledge and transformation.

What Did We Learn?

! Arctic wolves are a subspecies of Gray wolves known for their large paws and thick coats.

! They live in packs consisting of 3 to 11 wolves and reach maturity once they are two years old.

! They can live in various habitats and hunt for many prey, such as rodents and rabbits (but they'll also consume berries and grass.)

! The Arctic wolf is known for its strength and endurance, which has given it the title of Super Wolf among many people.

Wolves mostly live in packs, but they can also live by themselves, making it difficult to determine what specific habitat is best for them. Their ability to hunt prey changes depending on the number of wolves in the pack, so their location changes based on available food sources. Still, some habitats are more common than others. Wolves are more likely to survive in areas with a wide range of habitats because they can adapt their behavior based on the pack's needs.

There Are a Variety of Wolf Habitats

Wolves are highly adaptable animals; they can easily live in forests, grasslands, mountains, tundra, deserts, and open plains. The increase in human development has led to wolves living close to humans and their settlements. Even in the wilderness, there is rarely a place where they cannot be found. Wolves are all across North America, Europe, Asia, and other continents.

Gray wolves tend to look for their home in forests and grasslands because they're ideal for survival.

Wolf in its habitat

One of the most important factors that determine how many wolves can live together is available food. Since they are carnivores, their diet consists mainly of meat, but they can also eat berries and vegetation. If there is plenty of prey, such as deer or rabbits, more wolves will survive in that area. If food is not plentiful, then fewer wolves may be able to survive. The pack size often varies depending on the available food and living conditions.

It is also very important that there is plenty of water for drinking – and bathing – where they live. Wolves like to keep clean and cool, especially in hot climates such as deserts or open plains. The size of the body of water also affects how many wolves are in that area. Larger bodies of water are more suitable for large packs, while smaller bodies of water are better for smaller packs.

Arctic Wolves have many open spaces and always stay close to bodies of water to hunt for food.

Arctic wolf hunting

Wolf Dens

Wolves typically live in dens that they construct themselves. In some areas, such as forests, they may dig their den into the ground. They will sometimes use caves or burrows that other animals have dug. In open plains and tundra, wolves often seek shelter from the wind and sun under overhanging rocks.

In deserts, they will occasionally dig their den into the side of a hill to help keep cool during the day. The shelter is usually large enough for an adult wolf and a litter of pups to sleep comfortably, but not much larger.

Depending on where a wolf lives, it can have many dens or just one. In general, wolves in the northern regions have more dens than those in warmer climates.

The Importance of Dens

Dens are very important in many ways. The pups stay in the den with their mother until they are old enough to hunt – typically when

Pups in a den

hey are about three months old. During this time, the female will ot leave her pups except for short hunting trips. Without the emale, the pack cannot hunt and therefore would not be able to urvive. The pups are also vulnerable to predators when they first eave the den because they have little defense against larger nimals such as bears, mountain lions, or humans.

When a mother wolf leaves the den to hunt, she will line it with soft rass and bedding to make it more comfortable for the pups. She ill also bring the meat and other bits of food that she obtains rom her hunting trips. Without their mother's protection, the ups would almost certainly die.

Wolves use several different dens depending on where they live nd what is most convenient at the time. They typically make one arge den for the entire pack. However, if only a few wolves are in he pack, they may have several different dens that they use for esting and giving birth.

What Did We Learn?

Wolves have adapted to a wide variety of habitats and can thrive in many different environments.

In general, they prefer to live in forests where there is plenty of food available. They also like places where the ground is soft so they can easily dig their dens. Wolves in deserts and open plains must find some type of shelter from the sun and heat.

Wolves love habitats where there is plenty of water for drinking and bathing.

Pups stay in the den for three months and are protected by their mothers.

Wolves are powerful, intelligent hunters, which explains why they are at the top of the food chain. Wolves are opportunistic feeders and can eat a large quantity of food when given a chance. When hunting solo or in small packs, wolves will stalk prey much smaller than them, such as rabbits and rodents. They may also scavenge the remains of large kills made by other predators or search for remains where they can find them.

Hunting Tactics

Wolves hunt in packs, helping each other chase prey into exhaustion. In other words, they run their prey and scare them into being so tired that they can no longer run or fight. Their hunting behavior depends highly on human intervention and food availability.

A wolf hunting

In Yellowstone National Park, wolves typically use a tactic called "surround and collect" when hunting big game animals such as elk, bison, and moose. The wolves work together to chase the prey into a tight circle and then slowly close in on them before making a final, deadly attack.

A wolf eating its prey

Wolves usually hunt during the night or early morning hours because their prey is less alert at these times. They have been seen hunting alone as well. In both cases, wolves will stalk their prey quietly before attacking. Once they have caught their quarry, wolves will try to kill the animal quickly by biting down on its neck.

Diet

Wolves are primarily meat-eaters. However, depending on what is available in their location, wolves will eat just about anything, including plants and vegetation, when prey is scarce. Wolves are also known to eat *carrion* (older dead animals) when there is not enough prey or they are unable to catch anything else. This includes carcasses of large animals killed by other predators, such as cougars, bears, and human hunters. Wolves prefer the meat of hoofed mammals, including moose, deer, bison, buffalo, elk, and caribou, but they will also eat smaller animals, such as beavers, hares, rabbits, ground squirrels, mice, and voles. They are even known to eat fish, including salmon, trout, and pike.

Wolves have been observed eating plants on rare occasions when they are unable to find meat at all. Diet preferences change depending on the environment of the wolf pack, so their prey and feeding habits closely depend on where the wolves live.

Territory

Wolves establish territories around areas that are rich with prey, such as forests, meadows, and tundra. They have been seen in mountains, rocky uplands, open forested areas, and vast, flat, treeless areas.

Wolves use all of their senses, including sight, sound, smell, and taste, to mark their territory. They will patrol the boundaries of their territory and use scent markings to let other wolves know that they are entering another pack's space. Wolves will howl at the moon and stars to communicate with other pack members and announce their presence and boundaries.

Wolves need more than just food and shelter; they also need space to roam. Packs fight for territory when members of different packs meet. The most dominant wolf will win the fight for a section of land, which may result in one losing its life if a superior opponent challenges it.

Alpha Wolves

Wolves are typically led by an alpha male and an alpha female. An *alpha wolf* is the dominant member of a pack, controlling the other wolves through displays of power. These displays include growling, snarling, snapping their jaws, exposing their teeth, chasing others away from food sources, barking at others to keep them in line with the rest of the pack, and forcing them to submit when he is in control.

Alpha wolves are typically older than other members in a pack and have been with the same pack for a long time. They usually lead hunts when killing large prey, such as elk or moose, but may give

A wolf hunting

younger wolves opportunities to hunt smaller animals before letting them lead a hunt.

If an alpha dies, the next most dominant wolf in the pack takes over and replaces them. The new leader may be challenged by other pack members, especially if more than one wolf believes it should be leading the pack. The wolves fight until one submits to another and gives up being the *top dog*.

Influence on the Environment

Wolves can impact how humans live by affecting livestock and hunting opportunities. Although it may seem like they are taking food away from humans, they are also reducing animal populations that can cause harm. Wolves help control vegetation by preying on species of animals that eat plants or trample them underfoot while roaming in search of more prey. This allows other plant species to grow without being disturbed so often, which provides many organisms with homes, food, and shelter.

What Did We Learn?

! Wolves make perfect hunters, and they use their keen senses to identify prey from miles away.

! Although their hunting tactics are similar to those of big cats, wolves are more closely related to dogs.

! Wolves establish territories around areas that are rich with prey, such as forests, meadows, and tundra.

! Wolves are led by an alpha male and an alpha female.

! Wolves are important in keeping a balance in the environment.

Chapter 5: Wolves in Myths and Legends

Wolves have long been considered canines of the devil, ghosts, and man-eaters. Today they are known to be peaceful creatures that only survive by eating meat when necessary. However, that wasn't always the case. Many stories tell of wolves taking on human form to trick and harm others, wolves that talked to humans and even fought them, and wolves with magical powers.

Wolves in Ancient Times

In ancient times, the wolf was believed to be a divine symbol of war and hate, something to be feared. Even today, we see strong reminders of these ideas, as many believe that werewolves – humans who can take on the form of a wolf –are still seen in some parts of the world. In addition, as recently as the early 19th century, people in France and Germany were put on trial for being werewolves!

Mythological wolves, such as Fenrir from Norse mythology and Charon from Greek mythology, have been used to scare children into behaving. Many myths have been told of the strength and fear caused by wolves. They were said to be man-eaters and strong beasts that could not be stopped, even by gods.

The She-Wolf, Romulus, and Remus

One such story tells of a she-wolf that saved two human infants from dying, nursed them as if they were her own, and raised them as her cubs. When the boys reached adulthood, they found a city and named it *Rome* - after themselves. Romulus killed his brother Remus for making fun of him.

Romulus then went on to create an army that soon became mighty. His loyal men took his surname, "Romulus," and swore to serve him forever. When he died, Romulus was made into a god and given his place among the stars.

Fenrir the Monstrous Wolf

Fenrir

One of the most famous wolves in mythology is Fenrir, a monstrous wolf that has been described as one of Loki's children. Loki, known for his clever mind and trickery, gave birth to this monster with *Angrboða* – a creature so hideous even the gods were afraid of her! Fenrir was later chained to a rock by the god Týr after being tricked into giving him his right hand. At Ragnarok, Fenrir is said to break free and feast on Odin's flesh.

Saint Francis and the Wolf

One story found in Italy tells of Saint Francis taming a wolf. This wolf was considered evil because it had attacked several people, including Saint Francis' brother. According to legend, Saint Francis was able to walk up to this wolf with nothing but his faith and tame it. He then brought the wolf to live with him in peace.

What Did We Learn?

! Although many may see wolves differently today, you can still find remnants of these myths in current culture.

! Romulus and his brother Remus were raised by a wolf and founded the city of Rome.

! Fenrir, the wolf child of Loki, was chained to a rock.

! Saint Francis, with faith alone, was able to tame a wolf and live with it peacefully.

There are countless stories associated with wolves. One of the most famous of these, as mentioned earlier, is the one about Romulus and Remus. Despite how powerful this myth has become in our culture, there are also some true stories about humans who have been raised by or have lived with wolves, *and their stories are just as incredible!*

The Tale of Dina Sanichar - The Real-Life Mowgli

One of the most incredible stories is of Dina Sanichar, who was raised by wolves in India. He was abandoned by his family in the jungles of Northern India when he was just three years old. He was raised by a family of wolves and – amazingly – learned to mimic

their behavior and communicate with them. He spent the first years of his life with the wolves, even living in a cave with them. By watching them, he learned to eat the same food they ate and followed their pack behavior. Eventually, he was discovered by some hunters who took him in.

Initially, when taken into care, Dina wouldn't sleep under a roof at night. Instead, he would climb a tree and sleep there until morning. He also refused to eat any of the food that was given to him. Instead, he tried to get his hands on some fruit from a nearby orchard. But over time, Dina adjusted and learned how to live with people again through education and training. He now lives with his human family but still spends some time living in the jungle where he grew up.

Shaun Ellis - The Wolf Man

Another incredible real-life wolf story is about Shaun Ellis, who decided to raise three wolf pups in the wild by pretending to be a wolf himself. Ellis, an English animal researcher and founder of Wolf Pack Management, has spent decades living among and studying wolves and has even been accepted as one of their own.

In 1993, he decided there was no better way to study these animals than by actually living among them. He decided he wouldn't eat anything except for what he could kill himself during his first year as a wolf. So, Ellis set out to find a pack of wolves.

Shunned by two packs, he was accepted into the third one and stayed with them for nine months before being forced to leave due to his reluctance to attack other animals in the wolf pack's territory. But he had been accepted as a pack member so much that he was accepted and given a second chance when he returned three years later.

He stayed with the pack in a region of Siberia for several months in what he called a "fantastic" experience that gave him rare insight into wolf behavior. He said that when you become one of them, they will accept you as one of their own, and his experiences taught him more about them than he had ever learned before.

While Ellis was incredibly grateful for the experience, it wasn't all easy. He was nearly attacked by an adult male once, and his new friends were often ill or would die of old age during his stay. Despite this, he considers the experience one of the best times in his life.

Kaspar Mansurov - The Real-Life Revenant

Another amazing story is Kaspar Mansurov, a Russian man raised by wolves in Siberia. He was originally found wandering the Siberian woods in July 2008 when he was just 13 years old. At this time, he had no language abilities whatsoever and couldn't even walk on his legs properly.

Without the use of language, Mansurov couldn't explain where he had come from or how he lived among wolves for so long. However, it was quickly discovered that he spent ten years living with a pack of wolves known to attack humans on sight. He adapted to their behavior patterns and got along with them, even caring for one of the pups as if it was his own.

As you can see, there are many amazing stories about individuals or children being raised by wolves. Some of them even managed to become accepted as a pack member and live among them for many years. From Dina to Shaun and even the real-life Revenant himself, they're all examples of what our bodies can adapt to as long as we have a will and a strong desire to survive.

Conclusion

Wolves are majestic and wild animals that are a wonder to learn about! The legacy of the wolf deserves to be told and remembered in all its glory, but we cannot do this without including the history of these wonderful creatures.

It's important to know that wolves are not only magnificent creatures worthy of our respect, but they also play an important role in maintaining a healthy ecosystem. Without them, many other species would suffer and die due to a lack of population control.

Wolves live in family units called packs, which usually consist of five to ten related individuals. However, very large packs consisting of up to thirty members exist. Packs are led by an alpha male and female who are the only ones permitted to mate within the pack structure. Along with their pups, the whole pack has a strict system in place to prevent fighting – unless an Alpha has died, and the position must be filled.

As apex predators, wolves play an important role in their ecosystems; they are at the top of the food chain and have few natural predators – humans are one. Men may hunt wolves or remove them from an area to prevent their attacks on livestock, even though human-wolf conflicts are rare.

Every one of the stories told about wolves in history is based on some kind of truth. And that's why it's important to recognize the true value of these creatures. They are more than just animals to be feared; they're creatures worthy of respect and honor.

References

Arctic Wolf Facts and Adaptations - Canis lupus arctos. (n.d.). Coolantarctica.Com. Retrieved from https://www.coolantarctica.com/Antarctica%20fact%20file/wildlife/Arctic_animals/arctic_wolf.php

DeLallo, L. (2011). Arctic wolf: The high arctic. Bearport Publishing.

Sinn, S. (2020, February 20). Wolf myths and folklore from around the world. Folklorethursday.Com. https://folklorethursday.com/myths/the-wolf-in-folklore-and-myth-around-the-world

Somervill, B. (2007). Gray Wolf. Cherry Lake Publishing. https://www.nwf.org/Educational-Resources/Wildlife-Guide/Mammals/Gray-Wolf

WolfWorlds. (2021, May 1). Wolf habitat - wolf facts and information. Wolfworlds.Com. https://www.wolfworlds.com/wolf-habitat

Printed in Great Britain
by Amazon

32791885R00030